PETEY

PETEY

by Tobi Tobias

paintings by Symeon Shimin

G. P. Putnam's Sons / New York

Text copyright © 1978 by Tobi Tobias
Illustrations copyright © 1978 by Symeon Shimin
All rights reserved. Published simultaneously in Canada by Longman,
Canada, Toronto. Printed in the United States of America.

Library of Congress Cataloging in Publication Data
Tobias, Tobi. Petey.
[1. Gerbils—Fiction. 2. Death—Fiction.] I. Shimin, Symeon II. Title
PZ7. T56Pe (E) 76-25515 ISBN 0-399-61044-8 lib. bdg.
Second Impression

for my daughter, Anne,
with everything

In the afternoon, like always, when I get home from school and say hello to Mom and check out what Benjy, my little brother, is up to and grab an apple, then I run upstairs and drop my school bag on my bed and see what my silly old gerbil, Petey, is doing. Usually he's banging this tin juice can he's so crazy about against the glass sides of his cage, making a whole song of happy clinks and clunks. He does it at night, too, and Daddy always says, when he comes in to kiss me, "How can you go to sleep with that racket?" but the real truth is I can hardly go to sleep without it. It's a friendly noise.

Or maybe he's building a fancy new nest for himself out of the cedar shavings and shredded burlap I put there for him. Or running himself dizzy in his exercise wheel. Or prying open a sunflower seed with his little paws and his tiny sharp teeth, or washing his funny mouse face or grooming his funny mouse tail. And then when he hears me (he really knows the sound of my voice), he stops what he's doing, sits up on his hind paws, looks around with his bright brown eyes, and I put my hand into the cage and he whisks right into it.

(7)

But this afternoon I get home late because it's my ice skating day. It's beginning to get dark in my room, and I can hardly see him. But then I do. He's all huddled up in a corner of his cage like he's shivering, and when I call out, "Petey, I'm home. Want a piece of apple? Want a sunflower seed?" he doesn't sit up, and right away I know something bad is going to happen.

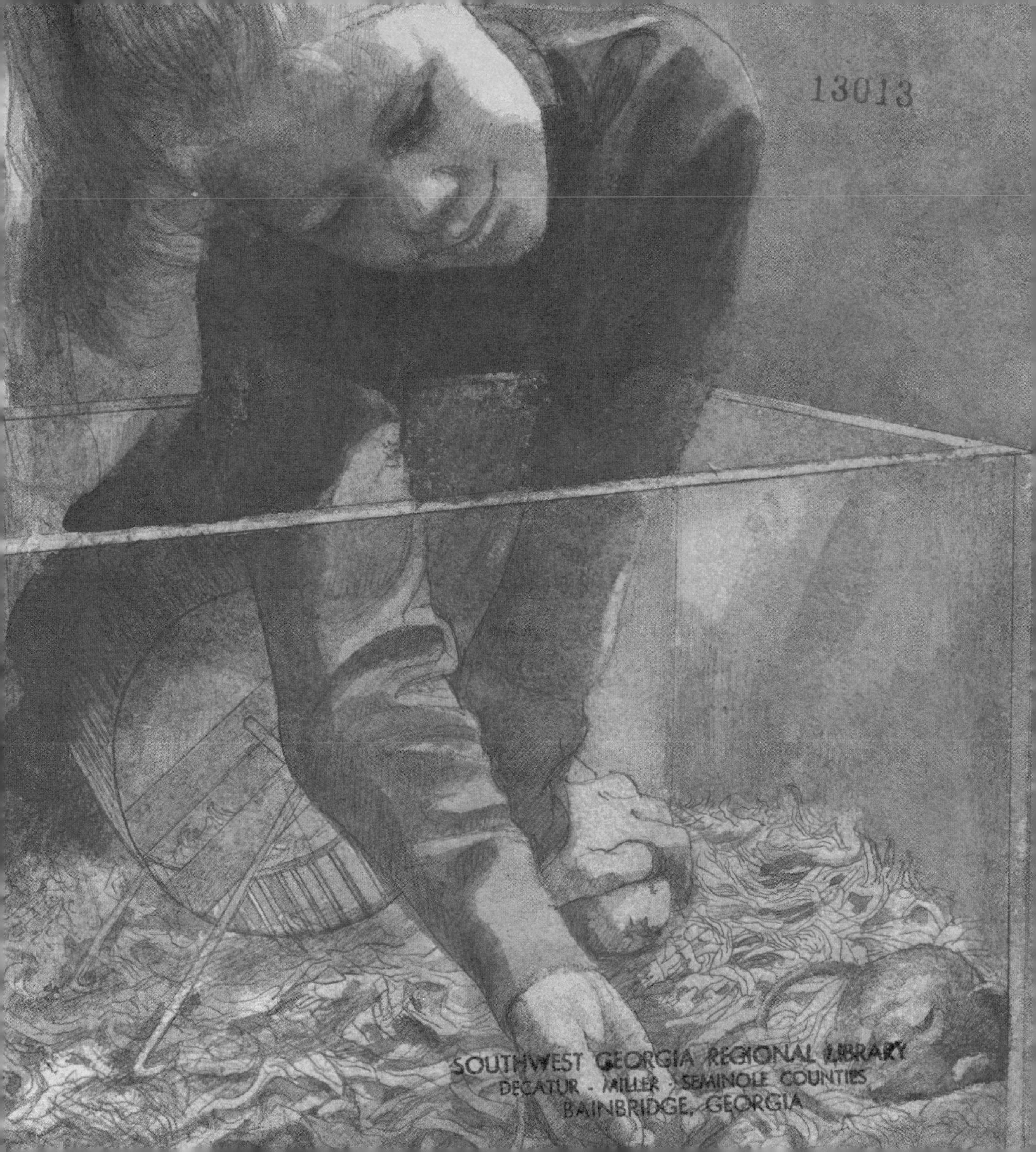

I call Daddy. That's how it is with me. For the everyday things I call Mommy. Sometimes she says I call her a hundred times a day. And for the one or two really scary things I call Daddy. And he comes and looks, and I can tell by his face what he's thinking is what I'm thinking too.

"Pete's sick, Emily," he says. And then comes the worst part. Very slowly, Daddy says, "You know, honey, Petey's almost five years old now and that's getting to be pretty old for a gerbil—"

"No," I say. Just "No."

"OK, Em," Daddy says. "Let's see what we can do for him."

So we look in the *How to Care for Your Pets* book we have, and it does not tell us any good news. You can't really doctor a gerbil, it says, you pretty much have to wait and see what happens. "If you have a sick gerbil one night," it says, "it's likely the next morning you'll either have a well gerbil or a dead gerbil." All I can say is the people who wrote that book must never have had a gerbil they loved or they wouldn't talk so smart.

Well, even if the book doesn't say anything you can do, we do everything we can think of. We change Petey's water, getting it just right between warm and cold, and we add a few drops of hamster medicine to it and try to coax Petey to drink. But he won't. Or maybe he can't. So we try plain water, because we think maybe he doesn't like the smell of the medicine, but Petey doesn't want that either. Then we shell some sunflower seeds and mash up the soft insides. I put the mash on my fingertip so Petey can lick it off. But he doesn't.

All the time we're doing this, Daddy is talking to me.

"Look at it this way, Em, Petey may be a well gerbil. The book says so. There's as much chance of that as—anything else."

"You were the one who said he was getting old," I yell, getting mad at him because I feel so terrible about Petey and not being able to do anything to help.

"Four or five years is a long life for a gerbil, Emmy. We've got to face up to that."

"It doesn't seem long to me," I say.

"Honey, think what a great time he's had with you. You've taken such good care of him. I don't just mean the feeding and keeping his cage clean. I mean all the talking and playing and loving."

Petey still won't take the food, and there is a long silence between the three of us.

After a while Daddy says, "Em, if someone's going to die, it's better this way. It really is. Sometimes when animals or people get old, their sickness comes on slowly, and it can be a very long time of hurting for them and everyone who loves them."

"Let's just be quiet," I say. "Maybe Petey's trying to sleep." But both of us know that Petey's never needed quiet for sleeping. Just the way I could sleep with his racket he could sleep with mine.

After supper Daddy and I are watching over Petey again, and Benjy comes in. "Here," he says, and he gives me a little piece off his sucking blanket. "For Petey." I fold it up like a little pillow and put it under Petey's head. Benjy is scared. "Is Petey going to die?" he asks Daddy.

"I'm afraid he is, Ben," Daddy says, "but we're still hoping he won't."

(16)

When I wake up in the middle of that night, it's still the same with Petey. I try the food and the water again, but he doesn't care. Then I try just sitting by his cage and stroking his soft, shiny fur with my finger. Even if it doesn't help, maybe he knows I'm there, and anyway I know I'm there, and that makes me feel a little better. After a while it gets cold sitting on the floor by Petey's cage, so I get back into my bed and pull up the covers the way Petey burrows into his nest of soft burlap and good-smelling shavings, and I think about how cute he was when he was a little baby, and I guess I finally fall asleep.

In the morning, right when I wake up, I don't remember for a minute, but then I do, and it hits me like someone threw a rock at my stomach. I go over to Petey's cage, very quietly. He's stretched out by his exercise wheel, not moving. I try to call Mommy and Daddy, but I haven't any voice left. I guess they know I need someone, though, and they come into my room. I forget which one of us says, "He's dead," but anyway I'm crying while Mommy holds me tight. I think she's crying a little, too.

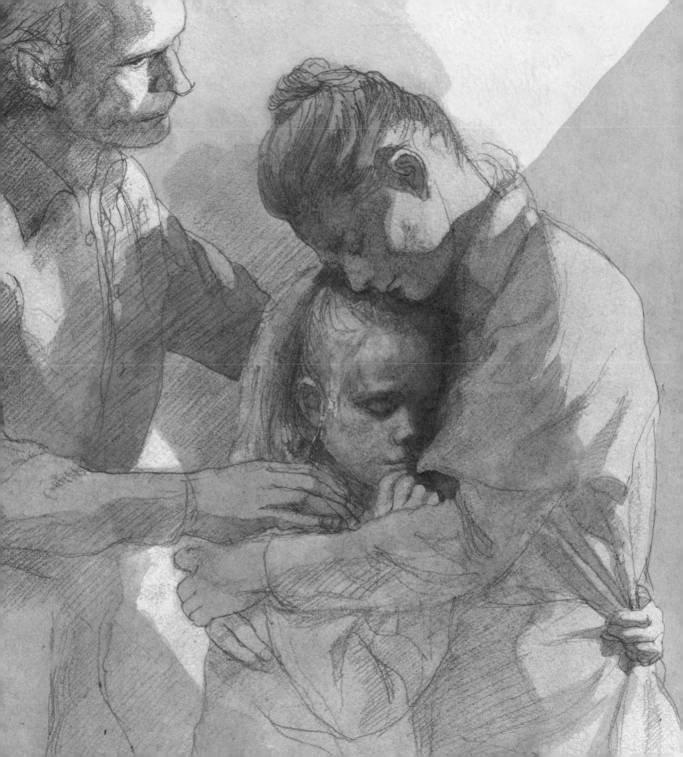

Then, all of a sudden, we start to talk about all the things we remember about him, all his little ways and tricks, and how smart and beautiful he was. We're telling each other the crazy adventures he's had, like the time he knocked the screen lid off his cage and ran away. We chased after him, but that must have scared him, and he wouldn't come out, and we couldn't find him anywhere. We finally found him on a shelf in the kitchen, curled up in a box of oatmeal, sleepy and full, with a funny look on his face, like he was laughing.

Then we have breakfast.

Afterward Mommy gets her best box — the one her silver birthday bracelet came in — and we put some colored tissue paper in it, and then she puts Petey in, very gently. We all give him good-bye pats, even Benjy, who's a little scared to.

We bury him in the back yard, just under where the shadow of the swing falls when it's swinging the highest.

I miss him. Every time I look at the empty cage I feel empty inside me. I miss him when Benjy finds a box of sunflower seeds and starts shelling them and eating the juicy insides. I miss him when Mommy scoops the frozen orange juice out of the tin can. I miss him when I see anything soft and shreddy that would be good to make a nest with. It's like things are all over the place, reminding me. Whenever I think about Petey, I love remembering all the good times we had, but then I feel awful because there won't be any more. Mostly I miss him when I'm going to sleep. It's so quiet.

It's starting to be spring now. I'm coming home from skating again, and Mommy's on the telephone. She says, "I'll ask her, Helen, and I'll let you know. Thanks a lot," and hangs up.

She says, "Hi," and, "Don't put those wet skates on the table," and gives me a kiss. I give her a wet apple kiss back. She says, "That was Helen," and she tells me that our friends Helen and George's two gerbils that they thought were brothers just had a litter of five babies, so one of them isn't. I laugh, and then I feel sad, because I think of Petey. Mommy says Helen and George know how bad I feel that Petey died, and they'd like to give me two of the babies when they're old enough to leave their mother.

I test out the idea in my head, but it doesn't feel too good. No one, no one could be like Petey. I say, "Not right now."

Mommy says, "No, not right now. But in a while."

I say, "It won't be the same."

Mommy says, "I never said it would be the same. It can be different, Em, and still be good."

I'm going to think it over and let her know.

(30)

TOBI TOBIAS lives with her husband, Irwin Tobias, and their children, Anne and John, in the brownstone they are renovating on New York's Upper West Side. Among her books for children are *A Day Off, Isamu Noguchi: The Life of a Sculptor,* and *The Quitting Deal.*

Ms. Tobias is a dance critic and an associate editor of *Dance Magazine.*

SYMEON SHIMIN is a well-known illustrator and a recognized painter. He has been invited to exhibit at the Whitney Museum, the Brooklyn Museum, the Art Institute of Chicago and the National Gallery in Washington, D.C., and his paintings are in public and private collections.

Mr. Shimin is the author and illustrator of the recent book *I Wish There Were Two of Me.*